PLAYING

RIGHT FIELD

PLAYING RIGHT FIELD

SCHOLASTIC INC.
New York Toronto London Auckland Sydney
Mexico City New Delhi Hong Kong

by Willy Welch
illustrated by
Marc Simont

ISBN 0-439-13994-5

12 11 10 9 8 7 6 5 4   2 3 4 5/0

Printed in the U.S.A.   14

First Scholastic Trade paperback printing, June 2000

Marc Simont used charcoal and watercolors to create the illustrations for this book.

Book design by Claire Counihan and Marc Simont

To Wendy, Grady, and
Molly Bess
— W.W.

To the members of
the Cornwall Consolidated School
baseball team
— M.S.

Saturday summers, when I was a kid,

we'd run to the school yard, and here's what we did.

We'd pick out the captains and choose up the teams.

It was always a measure of my self-esteem

because the strongest and fastest played shortstop and first.

The last ones they picked were the worst.

I never needed to ask. It was sealed.

I just took up my place in right field.

Playing right field, it's easy, you know.

You can be awkward and you can be slow.

That's why I'm here in right field

watching the dandelions grow.

Playing right field can be lonely and dull.

Little Leagues never have lefties that pull.

I'd dream of the day they'd hit one my way.
They never did. But still I would pray
that I'd make a fantastic catch on the run
and not lose the ball in the sun.

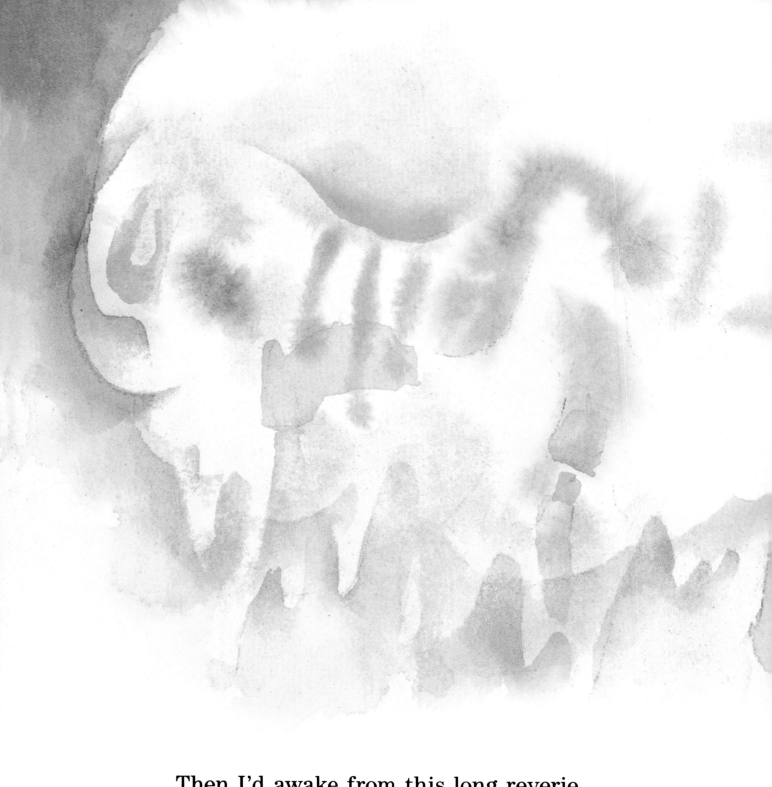

Then I'd awake from this long reverie

and pray that the ball never came out to me.

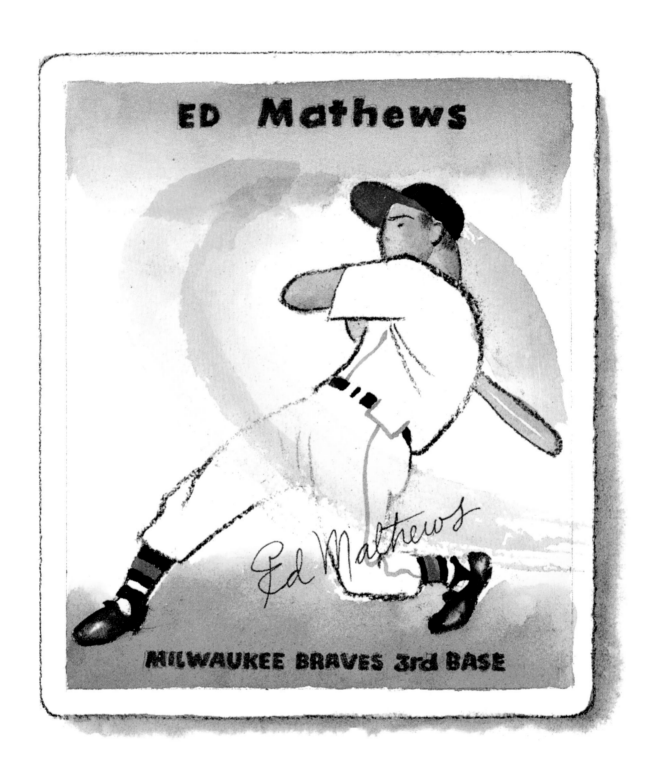

Sometimes I'd dream I was Mathews or Mays
hitting home runs and making great plays.

But they were so graceful, and they were so fast;
they never batted last.

Off in the distance, the game's dragging on.

There are strikes on the batter; some runners are on.

I don't know the inning. I've forgotten the score.

The whole team is yelling and I don't know what for.

Suddenly everyone's looking at me.

My mind has been wandering. What could it be?

They point to the sky and I look up above.

And a baseball falls into my glove!

Here in right field, it's important, you know.

You've got to know how to catch.

You've got to know how to throw.

That's why I'm here in right field

watching the dandelions grow.